G186s

Garner.
The stone book.

DATE DUE

NOV 28 '90			

THE
STONE BOOK

ALAN GARNER

Etchings by Michael Foreman

COLLINS

Library of Congress Cataloging in Publication Data

Garner, Alan
   The stone book.

   SUMMARY: His daughter's request for a book
prompts a stonemason to reveal the secret of the
stone to her.
      [1.   Fathers and daughters—Fiction]
I.   Foreman, Michael, 1938-   II.   Title.
PZ7.G18417St   1978   [Fic.]   78-7965
ISBN 0-529-05503-1

First United States edition published 1978 by
William Collins + World Publishing Company,
New York and Cleveland.

Originally published in 1976 by
William Collins Sons & Co., Ltd., London and
Glasgow. All rights reserved. Printed in
the United States of America.

FOREWORD

The Stone Book is one of a quartet of books by Alan
Garner. The other titles are *Granny Reardun, The
Aimer Gate,* and *Tom Fobble's Day.* Each book stands
on its own, but together they form a saga tracing four
generations of a working class family in Chorley, a
small town in Cheshire, England.

In *The Stone Book* we meet Mary and her
stonemason father; Mary's son is Joseph, the "granny
reardun" of the second book; Robert, the boy who
thinks he might become a soldier like his Uncle
Charley in *The Aimer Gate,* is Joseph's son; and
William, whose sled is "Tom Fobbled" in the final
book, is Joseph's grandson. The first book is set in
Victorian England; the last takes place during World
War II.

Alan Garner grew up in the area of England in
which the quartet is set, and he has a deep familiarity
with the people of whom he writes. The simplicity of
his style in these books is meticulous, poetic—and
perfectly suited to their universal and deeply moving
themes. For beneath the surface of the stories, which
are engrossing in themselves, the author probes the

mysteries of his characters' linkage with their
ancestors and with the deeper past. They search for
their individual identities; they meet danger with
courage; they mitigate poverty with humor; they
experience love and joy; and they face with stoicism
the inevitability of death. The books, though brief
and unpretentious, have an elemental universality
rather like Greek plays, which indeed have been very
much a part of Alan Garner's literary background.

The language he has chosen to use is a combination
of modern English with the old northwest Mercian
spoken pattern. Many words from the past are still
in everyday use in rural Cheshire, and Garner uses them
without apology or explanation in the books. This may
give some readers pause, but their use is so natural
that their meaning is obvious, and they deepen and
enrich both the credibility and the power of the books.

For Glenda and Stephan
whose father found
the stone book

THE
STONE BOOK

A bottle of cold tea, bread and a half onion.
That was Father's baggin. Mary emptied her
apron of stones from the field and wrapped the
baggin in a cloth.

The hottest part of the day was on. Mother
lay in bed under the rafters and the thatch,
where the sun could send only blue light. She
had picked stones in the field until she was too
tired and had to rest.

Old William was weaving in the end room. He had to weave enough cuts of silk for two markets, and his shuttle and loom rattled all the time, in the day and the night. He wasn't old, but he was called Old William because he was deaf and hadn't married. He was Father's brother.

He carried the cuts to market on his back. Stockport was further, but the road was flatter. Macclesfield was nearer, but Old William had to climb Glaze Hill behind the cottage to get to the road. The markets were on Tuesday and Friday, and so he was weaving and walking always: weave and walk. "Then where's time for wedding?" he used to say.

Mary opened the door of Old William's room. "Do you want any baggin?" she said. She didn't speak, but moved her lips to shape the words.

"A wet of a bottle of tea," said Old William. He didn't speak, either. The loom was too loud. Mary and Old William could talk when everybody else was making a noise.

"Is it sweet?" he said.

"Yes. I made it for Father."

"Where's he working?"

"Saint Philip's," said Mary.

"Haven't they finished that steeple yet?" said Old William.

"He's staying to finish. They want it for Sunday."

"Tell him to be careful, and then. There's many another Sunday."

Old William was careful. Careful with weaving, careful carrying. He had to be. The weight could break his back if he fell on the hill.

"Mother!" Mary shouted up the bent stairs. "I'm taking Father his baggin!"

She walked under the trees of the Wood Hill along the edge of Lifeless Moss.

The new steeple on the new church glowed in the sun; but something glinted. The spire, stone like a needle, was cluttered with the masons' platforms that were left. All the way under the Wood Hill, Mary watched the

13

golden spark that had not been there before.

She reached the brick cottage on the brink of the Moss. Between there and the railway station were the houses that were being built. The railway had fetched a lot of people to Chorley. Before, Father said, there hadn't been enough work. But he had made gateposts, and the station walls, and the bridges and the Queen's Family Hotel; and he had even cut a road through rock with his chisel, and put his mark on it. Every mason had his mark, and Father put his at the back of a stone, or on its bed, where it wouldn't spoil the facing. But when he cut the road on the hill, he put his mark on the face once, just once, to prove it.

Then Chorley must have a church next, and a school.

Father had picked the site for the quarry at the bottom of the Wood Hill. Close by the place, at the road, there was stone to be seen, but it was the soft red gangue that wouldn't last ten years of weather. Yet Father had looked at the way the trees grew, and had felt the earth and the leaf mold between his fingers, and had said they must dig there. And there they had found the hard yellow-white dimension stone that was the best of all sands for building.

The beech trees had been cleared over a space, and two loads of the big branches had saved them coals at home for a year. It was one of the first memories of her life: the rock bared and cut by Father, and silver bark in the fire.

Now the quarry seemed so small, and the church so big. The quarry would fit inside a corner of the church; but the stone had come from it. People said it was because Father cut well, but Father said that a church was only a bit of stone round a lot of air.

Mary stood at the gate and looked up. High clouds moving made the steeple topple towards her.

"Father!"

She could hear his hammer, *tac, tac,* as he combed the stone.

15

The golden spark was a weathercock. It had been put up that week, and under its spike was the top platform. Father's head showed over the edge of the platform.

"Below!" His voice sounded nearer than he looked.

"I've brought your baggin!" Mary shouted.

"Fetch it, then!"

"All the way?"

"Must I come down when I'm working?"

"But what about the Governor?" said Mary.

"He's gone! I'm the Governor of this gang! There's only me stayed to finish! Have you the tea?"

"Yes!"

"Plenty of sugar?"

"Yes!"

"I can't spit for shouting! Come up!"

Mary hitched her frock and put the knot of the baggin cloth between her teeth and climbed the first ladder.

The ladders were spiked and roped, but the beginning of the steeple was square, a straight

16

drop, and the ladders clattered on the side. She didn't like that.

"Keep fast hold of that tea!" she heard Father call, but she didn't lift her head, and she didn't look down.

Up she went. It felt worse than a rock because it was so straight and it had been made. Father had made parts of it. She knew the pattern of his combing hammer on the sandstone.

Up she went.

"Watch when you change to the spire!" Father's voice sounded no nearer.

At the spire, the pitch of the ladders was against the stone, and Mary had to step sideways to change. The ladders were firmer, but she began to feel a breeze. She heard an engine get up steam on the railway. The baggin cloth kept her mouth wet, but it felt dry.

The spire narrowed. There were sides to it. She saw the shallow corners begin. Up and up. *Tac, tac, tac, tac,* above her head. The spire narrowed. Now she couldn't stop the blue sky from showing at the sides. Then land. Far away.

Mary felt her hands close on the rungs, and her wrists go stiff.

Tac, tac, tac, tac. She climbed to the hammer. The spire was thin. Father was not working, but giving her a rhythm. The sky was now inside the ladder. The ladder was broader than the spire.

Father's hand took the baggin cloth out of Mary's mouth, and his other hand steadied her as she came up through the platform.

The platform was made of good planks, and Father had lashed them, but it moved. Mary didn't like the gaps between. She put her arms around the spire.

"That was a bonny climb," said Father.

"I do hope the next baby's a lad," said Mary.

"Have some tea," said Father.

She drank from the bottle. The cold sweet drink stopped her trembling.

"Don't look yet," said Father. "And when you do, look away first, not near. How's Mother?"

"Resting. She could only do five hours at the picking today; it got that hot."

"That's why I've stayed," said Father. "They want us to finish for Sunday, and there's one more dab of capping to do. There may be a sixpence for it."

"Doesn't it fear you up here?" said Mary.

"Now why should it?" said Father. "Glaze Hill's higher."

"But you can't fall off Glaze Hill," said Mary. "Not all at once."

"There's nothing here to hurt you," said Father. "There's stone, and wood, and rope, and sky, same as at home. It's the same ground."

"It's further," said Mary.

"But it'll never hurt. And I'll go down with you. Down's harder."

"I hope the next one's a lad," said Mary. "I'm fed up with being a lad—Father! See at the view! Isn't it!''

Mary stood and looked out from the spire. "And the church,'' she said. "It's so far away.'' She knelt and squinted between the planks. "The roof's as far as the ground. We're flying.''

Father watched her; his combing hammer swung from his arm.

"There's not many who'll be able to say they've been to the top of Saint Philip's.''

"But I'm not at the top,'' said Mary.

The steeple cap was a swelling to take the socket for the spike of the golden cockerel. Mary could touch the spike. Above her the smooth belly raced the clouds.

"You're not frit?''

"Not now,'' said Mary. "It's grand.''

Father picked her up. "You're really not frit? Nobody's been that high. It was reared from the platform.''

"Not if you help me,'' said Mary.

"Right,'' said Father. "He could do with a testing. Let's see if he runs true.''

Father lifted Mary in his arms, thick with work from wrist to elbow. For a moment again the steeple wasn't safe on the earth when she felt the slippery gold of the weathercock bulging over her, but she kicked her leg across its back, and held the neck.

"Get your balance," said Father.

"I've got it," said Mary.

The swelling sides were like a donkey, and behind her the tail was stiff and high. Father's head was at her feet, and he could reach her.

"I'm set," she said.

Father's face was bright, and his beard danced. He took off his cap and swept it in a circle and gave the cry of the summer fields.

"Who-whoop! Wo-whoop! Wo-o-o-o!"

Mary laughed. The wind blew on the spire and made the weathercock seem alive. The feathers of its tail were a marvel.

Father twisted the spike with his hands against the wind, and the spike moved in its greased socket, shaking a bit, juddering, but firm. To Mary the weathercock was waking.

The world turned. Her bonnet fell off and hung by its ribbon, and the wind filled her hair.

"Faster! Faster!" she shouted. "I'm not frit!" She banged her heels on the golden sides, and the weathercock boomed.

"Who-whoop! Wo-whoop! Wo-o-o-o!" cried Father. The high note of his voice crossed parishes and townships. Her hair and her bonnet flew, and she felt no spire, but only the brilliant gold of the bird spinning the air.

Father swung the tail as it passed him. *"Who-whoop! Wo-whoop! Wo-o-o-o!* There's me tip-top pickle of the corn!"

Mary could see all of Chorley, the railway and the new houses. She could have seen home but the Wood Hill swelled and folded into Glaze Hill between. She could see the cottage at the edge of Lifeless Moss, and the green of the Moss, and as she spun, she could see Lord Stanley's, and Stockport and Wales, and Beeston and Delamere, and all to the hills and Manchester. The golden twisting spark with the girl on top, and everywhere across the plain were churches.

"Churches! I can see churches!"

And all the weathercocks turned in the wind.

Father let the spike stop, and lifted her down.

"There," he said. "You'll remember this day, my girl. For the rest of your life."

"I already have," said Mary.

Father ate his baggin. Mary walked round the platform. She looked at the new vicarage and the new school by the new church.

"Are you wishing?" said Father.

"A bit," said Mary. "I'm wishing I'd went."

"It'd be fourpence a week, and all the time you'd have lost."

"I could have read," said Mary. "You can read."

She sat with her back against the steeple in its narrow shade. Glaze Hill was between her boots. "Have you asked if Lord Stanley'll set me on?''

"Lord Stanley doesn't like his maids to read," said Father.

"But have you?''

"Wait a year.''

"I'm fretted with stone picking," said Mary. "I want to live in a grand house, and look after every kind of beautiful thing you can think of—old things, brass.''

"By God, you'll find stone picking's easier!'' The onion dropped off Father's knife and thumb and floated down to the lawns of the church. It had so far to fall that there was time for it to wander in the air.

"We'd best fetch that," said Father. "The vicar won't have us untidy.''

He put Mary on the ladder and climbed outside her. Just as the sky and the steeple were inside the ladder, Mary was inside Father's long arms that pushed him out from the rungs. He didn't help her, but she felt free and safe and climbed as if there was no sky, no stone, no height.

She ran across the lawn and picked up the onion. Bits of it had smashed off, and she nibbled them.

She stood with Father and looked up. The spire still toppled under the clouds.

"She'll do," said Father, and slapped the stone. "Yet she'll never do."

"Why?" said Mary.

"She's no church, and she'll not be. You want a few dead uns against the wall for it to be a church."

"They'll come."

"Not here," said Father. "There's to be no burial ground. Just grass. And without you've some dead uns, it's more like Chapel than Church. Empty."

He ate his onion.

Mary went back to work. She looked at Saint Philip's when she got to Lifeless Moss. Father was nearly at the top again. His arms were straight. He climbed balanced out from the stone.

She dipped a pansion of water in the spring

and took some up to Mother. Mother was sleeping, but her hair was flat with sweat.

Old William was sweating at his loom. It was all clack. He had to watch the threads, and he couldn't look to talk.

Mary worked till the sun was cool; then she carried her stones home and made the tea. She washed little Esther and put her to bed, and gave Mother her tea. Father came home.

"That's finished," he said. He sat quietly in his chair. He was always quiet when the work was done, church or wall or garden.

After tea, Father went to see Mother. They talked, and he played his ophicleide to her. He played gentle tunes, not the ones for Sunday.

Mary cleared the table and washed the dishes. And when she'd finished, she cleaned the stones from the field. Old William smoked half a pipe of tobacco before going back to the loom.

"Is he playing?" said Old William.

"Yes," said Mary. "But not Chapel. Why

27

are we Chapel?''

"You'd better ask him," said Old William. "I'm Chapel because it's near. I do enough walking, without Sunday."

Father came down from playing his music. He sat at the table with Mary and sorted the stones she had picked that day with little Esther. Most pickers left their stones on the dump at the field end, but Mary brought the best of hers home and cleaned the dirt off, and Father looked at them. In the field they were dull and heavy, and could break a scythe; but on the table each one was something different. They were different colors and different shapes, different in size and feel and weight. They were all smooth cobbles.

"Why are we Chapel?" said Mary.

"We're buried Church," said Father.

"But why?"

"There's more call on music in Chapel," said Father.

"Why?"

"Because people aren't content with raung-

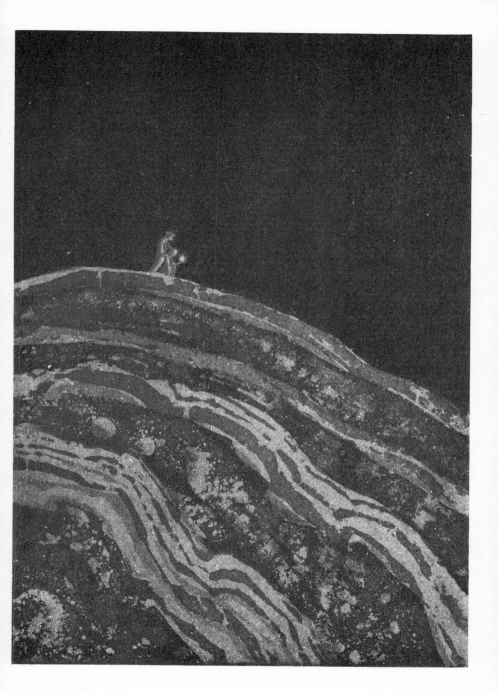

ing theirselves to death from Monday to Saturday, but they must go bawling and praying and fasting on Sundays too.''

"What's the difference between Church and Chapel?" said Mary.

"Church is Lord Stanley."

"Is that all?"

"It's enough," said Father. "When you cut stone, you see more than the parson does, Church or Chapel."

"Same as what?"

"Same as this." Father took a stone and broke it. He broke it cleanly. The inside was green and grey. He took one half and turned so that Mary couldn't see how he rubbed it. Mary had tried to polish stone, but a whole day of rubbing did no good. It was a stone-cutter's secret, one of the last taught. Father held the pebble inside his waistcoat, and whatever it was that he did was simple—a way of holding, or twisting. And the pebble came out with its broken face green and white flakes, shining like wet.

He gave the pebble to Mary.

"Tell me how those flakes were put together and what they are," he said. "And who made them into pebbles on a hill, and where that was a rock and when." He rummaged in the pile on the table, found a round, grey stone, broke it, turned away, held, twisted, rubbed. "There."

Mary cried out. It was wonderful. Father had polished the stone. It was black and full of light, and its heart was a golden, bursting sun.

"What is it?" said Mary.

"Ask the parson," said Father.

"But what is it really?"

"I can't tell you," said Father. "Once, when I was 'prenticed, we had us a holiday, and I walked to the sea. I left home at two in the morning. I had nothing but half an hour there. And I stood and watched all that water, and all the weeds and shells and creatures; and then I walked back again. And I've seen the like of what's in that pebble only in the sea. They call them urchins. Now you tell me how that urchin got in that flint, and how that flint got on that hill."

"Was it Noah's flood?" said Mary.

"I'm not saying. But parsons will tell you, if you ask them, that Heaven and Earth, center and circumference, were created all together in the same instant, four thousand and four years before Christ, on October the twenty-third, at nine o'clock in the morning. They've got it written. And I'm asking parsons, if it was Noah's flood, where was the urchin before? How long do stones take to grow? And how do urchins get in stones? It's time and arithmetic I want to know. Time and arithmetic and sense."

"That's what comes of reading," said Old William. "You're all povertiness and discontent, and you'll wake Mother."

"And what are you but a little master?" said Father. "Weaving till all hours and nothing to show for what you've spent."

"I'm still a man with a watch in his pocket,"

said Old William. "I don't keep my britches up with string."

Mary slid under the table and held on to the flint. There was going to be a row. Father thought shouting would make Old William hear, and Old William didn't have Father's words. Old William's clogs began to move as if he was working the loom, and Father's boots became still as if there was a great stone in his lap. Although he shouted, anger made him calm. When he was so still, he frightened Mary. It was worse when the stillness came from himself and his thoughts, without a row. Sometimes it lasted for days. Then he would go out and play his ophicleide around the farms, and sing, and ring his handbells, and use all his music for beer, and only Mother could fetch him home. That was what Mary feared the most, because beer took Father beyond himself and left someone looking through his eyes.

"And what about the cost of candles?" said Old William. "Books are dear reading when you've bought them."

Mary held the flint and tried to imagine such a golden apple that was once a star beneath the sea.

"Get weaving," said Father, "or it's you'll be the poverty-knocker."

Old William's clogs went out. Father sat at the table, not even moving the stones. Then he stood up and walked into the garden. Mary waited. She heard him rattling the hoe and rake, and Old William started up his loom, but she could tell he was upset, because of the slow beat, "Plenty-of-time, plenty-of-time." She crawled from under the table and went out to the garden. Father was hoeing next to the rhubarb.

"If I can't learn to read, will you give me something instead?" said Mary.

"If it's not too much," said Father. "The trouble with him is," he said, and jutted his clay pipe at Old William's weaving room, "he's as good as me, but can't ever see the end of his work. And I make it worse by building houses for the big masters who've taken his living. That's what it is, but we never say.''

''If I can't read, can I have a book?''

Father opened his mouth and the clay pipe fell to the ground and didn't break. He looked at the pipe. ''I have not seen a Macclesfield dandy that has fallen to the ground and not broken,'' he said. ''And they don't last more than a threeweek.'' He turned the soil gently with his hoe and buried the pipe.

''What've you done that for?'' said Mary. ''They cost a farthing!''

''Well,'' said Father, ''I reckon, what with all the stone, if I can't give a bit back, it's a poor do. Why a book?''

''I want a prayer book to carry to Chapel,'' said Mary. ''Lizzie Allman and Annie Leah have them.''

''Can they read?''

''No. They use them to press flowers.''

''Well, then,'' said Father.

''But they can laugh,'' said Mary.

"Ay," said Father. He leant on the hoe and looked at Glaze Hill. "Go fetch a bobbin of bad ends: two boxes of lucifer matches and a bundle of candles—a whole fresh bundle. We're going for a walk. And tell nobody."

Mary went into the house to Old William's room. In a corner by the door he kept the bad ends wound on bobbins. They were lengths of thread that came to him knotted or too thick or that broke on the loom. He tied them together and wove them for Mother to make clothes from. Mary lifted a bobbin and took it out. She found the candles and the lucifer matches.

Father had put his tools away.

They went up the field at the back of the house and onto Glaze Hill. When they reached the top, the sun was ready for setting. The weathercock on Saint Philip's was losing light, and woods stretched out.

"I can't see the churches," said Mary. "When we were up there this afternoon I could."

"That's because they're all of a height," said Father. "I told you Glaze Hill was higher."

Glaze Hill was the middle of three spurs of land. The Wood Hill came in from the right, and Daniel Hill from the left, and they met at the Engine Vein. The Engine Vein was a deep crevice in the rocks, and along it, went the tramroad for the miners who dug galena, cobalt and malachite. The thump of the engine that pumped water out of the Vein could often be heard through the ground on different parts of the hill, when the workings ran close to the surface.

Now it was dusk, and the engine quiet. The tramroad led down to the head of the first stope, and there was a ladder for men to climb into the cave.

Mary was not allowed at the Vein. It killed at least once every year, and even to go close was dangerous, because the dead sand around the edge was hard and filled with little stones that slipped over the crag.

Father walked on the sleepers of the tram-road down into the Engine Vein.

"It's nearly night," said Mary. "It'll be dark."

"We've candles," said Father.

There was a cool smell, and draughts of sweet air. The roof of the Vein began, and they were under the ground. Water dripped from the roof onto the sandstone, splashing echoes. The drops fell into holes. They had fallen for so many years in the same place that they had worn the rock. Mary could get her fingers into some of the holes, but they were deeper than her hands.

Above and behind her, Mary saw the last of the day. In front and beneath was the stope, where it was always night.

Father took the whole bundle of candles and set them on the rocks and lit them. They showed how dark it was in the stope.

"Wait while you get used to it," said Father. "You soon see better. Now what about that roof?"

Mary looked up into the shadows. "It's not dimension stone," she said. "There's a grain to it, and it's all ridge and furrow."

"But if you'd been with me that day," said Father, "when I was 'prenticed and walked to the sea, you'd have stood on sand just the same as that. The waves do it, going back and to. And it makes the ridges proper hard, and if you left it I reckon it could set into stone. But the tide goes back and to, back and to, and wets it. And your boots sink in and leave a mark."

"If that's the sea, why's it under the ground?" said Mary.

"And whose are those boots?" said Father.

There were footprints in the roof, flattening the ripples, as though a big bird had walked there.

"Was that Noah's flood, too?" said Mary.

"I can't tell you," said Father. "If it was, that bantam never got into the ark."

"It must've been as big as Saint Philip's cockerel," said Mary.

40

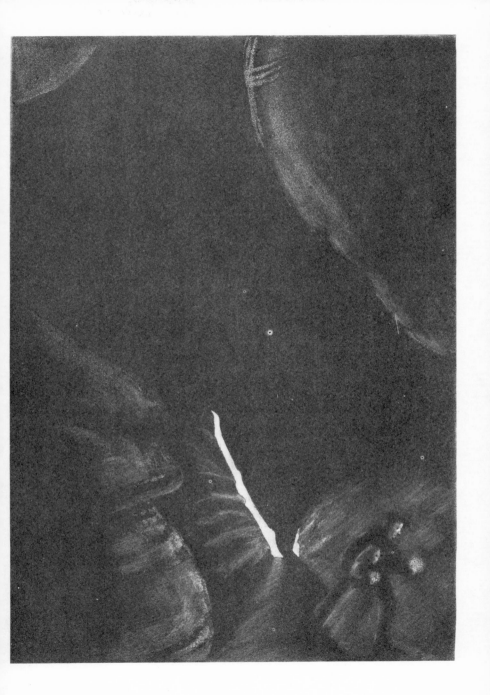

"Bigger," said Father. "And upside down."

"It doesn't make sense," said Mary.

"It would if we could plunder it deep enough," said Father. "I reckon that if you're going to put the sea in a hill and turn the world over and let it dry, then you've got to be doing before nine o'clock in the morning. But preachers aren't partial to coming down here, so it doesn't matter. Does it?"

He blew out all the candles except two. He gave one to Mary and stepped onto the ladder. Mary went with him, and climbed between his arms down into the stope.

"It'd take some plucking," she said.

"If it had feathers."

The stope was the shape of a straw beehive, and tunnels led everywhere. Mary couldn't see the top of the ladder.

"If you'd fallen, you'd have been killed dead as at Saint Philip's," said Father.

"It's different," said Mary. "There's no height."

"There's depth, and that's no different

than height," said Father.

"It doesn't call you," said Mary.

Father held Mary's hand sailor's grip and went into a tunnel under a ledge at the bottom of the stope. They didn't go far. There was a shaft in the rock, not a straight one, but when Father bridged it with his feet, the pebbles rattled down for a long time. It was easy climbing, even with a candle to be held, because the rock kept changing, and each change made a shelf. There was puddingstone, marl, and foxbench, and only the marl was slippery.

"That's it," said Father. They were at a kink in the shaft.

"What about further down?" said Mary.

"It's only rubbish gangue from here to the bottom—neither use nor ornament. Although there was a man, him as sank this shaft, and he could read books and put a letter together. But he lost his money, for all his reading. Now if he'd read rocks instead of books, it might have been a different story, you see."

Father held his candle out to the side. There was a crack, not a tunnel. The rock itself had made it.

"Hold fast to your light," said Father. "And keep the matches out of the wet."

Father had to crawl. Mary could stand, but even she had to squeeze, because of the narrowness.

The crack went up and down, wavering through the hill. Then Father stopped. He couldn't turn his head to speak, but he could crouch on his heel. "Climb over," he said.

Mary pulled herself across his back. A side of wall had split off and jammed in the passage, almost closing it.

"Can you get through there?" said Father.

"Easy," said Mary.

"Get through and then listen," said Father.

Mary wriggled past the flake and stood up. The passage went on beyond her light. Father's candle made a dark hole of where she had come, and she could see his boots and one hand. He pushed the bobbin of bad ends through to her, and six candles. He kept hold of the loose end of silk.

"What's up?" said Mary. "What are we doing?"

"You still want a book for Sundays?" said Father. "Even if you can't read?"

"Yes," said Mary.

"Then this is what we're doing," said Father. "So you listen. You're to keep the lucifers dry, and use only one candle. It should be plenty. Let the silk out, but don't pull on it, else it'll snap. It's to fetch you back if you've no light, and that's all it's for. Now then. You'll find you go down a bit of steep, and then the rock divides. Follow the malachite. Always follow the malachite. Do you understand me?"

"Yes, Father."

"After the malachite, there's some old foxbench, then a band of white dimension, and a lot of wet when you come to the Tough Tom. Can you remember it all?"

"Malachite, foxbench, dimension, Tough

45

Tom," said Mary.

"Always follow the malachite," said Father. "And if there's been another rockfall, don't trust loose stuff. And think on: there isn't anybody can reach you. You're alone."

"What must I do when I get to the Tough Tom?" said Mary.

"You come back and tell me if you want that book," said Father. "And if you do, you shall have it."

"Right," said Mary.

The crack in the hill ran straight for a while and was easier than the first part. She held her candle in one hand and the bobbin in the other. She had tucked the other candles and the lucifer matches into her petticoat. She went slowly down the rock, and the silk unwound behind her.

The steep was not enough to make her climb, and water trickled from above, over the rock, and left a green stain of malachite. She stopped when the passage divided, but there was nothing to worry her. She went to

dimension stone. And the crack finished at the end of her candlelight.

"Father!"

There was no reply. She hadn't counted how much silk had unwound.

"Father!"

There was plenty of candle left, but it showed her nothing to explain why she was there.

"Father!"

Not even an echo. There wasn't the room for one. But she turned. There hadn't been an echo, but her voice had sounded louder beyond the Tough Tom.

Mary scrambled up the hump, slithering in the wet. Then she looked around her, and saw.

The end of the crack was as broad as two stalls and as high as a barn. The red Tough Tom was a curved island above its own water. The walls were white and pale yellow. There was no sound. The water did not drip. It sank through the stone unheard, and seeped along the marl.

Mary saw Father's mason mark drawn on the wall. It was faint and black, as if drawn with soot. Next to it was an animal, falling. It had nearly worn itself away, but it looked like a bull, a great shaggy bull. It was bigger than it seemed at first, and Father's mark was on it, making the mark like a spear or an arrow.

The bull was all colors, but some of the stone had shed itself in the damp air. The more Mary looked, the bigger the bull grew. It had turned around every wall, as if it was moving and dying.

Mary had come through the hill to see Father's mark on a daubed bull. And near the bull and the mark, there was a hand, the outline of a hand. Someone had splayed a hand on the wall and painted round it with the Tough Tom. Fingers and thumb.

Mary put the candle close. A white dimension hand. She lifted her own and laid it over the hand on the wall, not touching. Both

50

hands were the same size. She reached nearer. They were the same size. She touched. The rock was cold, but for a moment it had almost felt warm. The hands fitted. Fingers and thumb and palm and a bull and Father's mark in the darkness under the ground.

Mary stood back, in the middle of the Tough Tom, and listened to the silence. It was the most secret place she had ever seen. A bull drawn for secrets. A mark and a hand alone with the bull in the dark that nobody knew.

She looked down. And when she looked down, she shouted. She wasn't alone. The Tough Tom was crowded. All about her in that small place under the hill that led nowhere were footprints.

They were the footprints of people, bare and shod. There were boots and shoes and clogs, heels, toes, shallow ones and deep ones, clear and sharp as if made altogether, trampling each other, hundreds pressed in the clay where only a dozen could stand. Mary was in a crowd that could never have been, thronging, as real as she was. Her feet made prints no fresher than theirs.

And the bull was still dying under the mark, and the one hand still held.

There was nowhere to run, no one to hear. Mary stood on the Tough Tom and waited. She daren't jerk the thread to feel Father's presence; he was so far away that the thread would have broken.

Then it was over. She knew the great bull on the rock enclosing her, and she knew the mark and the hand. The invisible crowd was not there, and the footprints in the Tough Tom churned motionless.

She had seen. Now there was the time to go. Mary lifted the thread and made skeins of it as she went past the white dimension, foxbench, and malachite to the candle under the fall.

Father had moved to make room for her.

"Well?"

"I've seen," said Mary. "All of it."

"You've touched the hand?"

"Yes."

"I thought you would."

They went back to the shaft, and up, and out. The sky seemed a different place. All things led to the bull and the mark and the hand in the cave. Trees were trying to find it with their roots. The rain in the clouds must fall to the ground and into the rock to the Tough Tom.

"That's put a quietness on you," said Father.

"Ay."

They came over Glaze Hill.

"Why did you set your mark on?" said Mary.

"I didn't. It was there when I went."

"When did you go?"

"When I was about your size. My father took me same as today. We have to go before we're too big to get past the fall, though I reckon, years back, the road was open—if you knew it was there."

"When did you go last?" said Mary.

"We go just once," said Father. "So that we'll know."

"Who else?"

"Only us. Neither Leahs nor Allmans. Us."

"But there were ever so many feet," said Mary. "The place was teeming."

"We've been going a while," said Father.

"And that bull," said Mary.

"That's a poser. There's been none like it in my time; and my father, he hadn't seen any."

"What is it all?" said Mary.

"The hill. We pass it on; and once you've seen it, you're changed for the rest of your days."

"Who else of us?" said Mary.

"Nobody," said Father, "except me; and now you. It's always been for the eldest; and from what I heard my father say, it was only ever for lads. But if they keep on stoping after that malachite the way they're going at the Engine Vein, it'll be shoveled up in a year or two without anybody noticing even. At one

56

time of day, before the Engine Vein and that chap who could read books, we must have been able to come at it from the top. But that's all gone. And if the old bull goes, you'll have to tell your lad, even if you can't show him.''

"I shall," said Mary.

"I recollect it puts a quietness on you, does that bull. And the hand. And the mark."

Mary went to wash the Tough Tom from her boots in the spring when they reached home. The spring came out of the hill and soaked into Lifeless Moss, and Lifeless Moss spilled by brooks to the sea.

Father sat with Mother for a while. Old William had picked up his usual rhythm, and the loom rattled, "Nickety-nackety, Monday-come-Saturday." Then Father collected his work tools and sat down at the table and sorted through the pebbles.

He weighed them in his hand, tested them on his thumbnail, until he found the one he wanted. He pushed the others aside; and he took the one pebble and worked quickly with candle and firelight, turning, tapping, knapping, shaping, twisting, rubbing and making, quickly, as though the stone would set hard if he stopped. He had to take the picture from his eye to his hand before it left him.

"There," said Father. "That'll do."

He gave Mary a prayer book bound in blue-black calfskin, tooled, stitched, and decorated. It was only by the weight that she could tell it was stone and not leather.

"It's better than a book you can open," said Father. "A book has only one story. And tomorrow I'll cut you a brass cross and let it in the front with some dabs of lead, and then I'll guarantee you'd think it was Lord Stanley's, if it's held right."

"It's grand," said Mary.

"And I'll guarantee Lizzie Allman and Annie Leah haven't got them flowers pressed in their books."

Mary turned the stone over. Father had split it so that the back showed two fronds of

a plant, like the silk in skeins, like the silk on the water under the hill.

And Father went out of the room and left Mary by the fire. He went to Old William and took his ophicleide, as he always did after shouting, and he played the hymn that Old William liked best because it was close to the beat of his loom. William sang for the rhythm, "Nickety-nackety, Monday-come-Saturday," and Father tried to match him on the ophicleide.

William bawled:

> "Oh, the years of Man are the looms
>   of God
> Let down from the place of the sun;
> Wherein we are weaving always,
> Till the mystic work is done!"

And so they ended until the next time. The last cry went up from the summer fields, *"Who-whoop! Wo-whoop! Wo-o-o-o!"*

And Mary sat by the fire and read the stone book that had in it all the stories of the world and the flowers of the flood.

About the Author

Alan Garner was born in a cottage at the foot of
Alderley Edge. Bedridden by an attack of meningitis, he
became a bookish child devouring Victorian literature.
The result was a scholarship to Manchester Grammar
School and later another to Oxford, where he studied
the Greek and Latin classics. Eventually, however,
he decided that university life was not the life he
wanted, so in 1957 he left Oxford to become a writer.
Today the critics have acclaimed him as a rare artist
and one of the most outstanding contemporary writers
of books for children. His earlier book, THE OWL
SERVICE, was the winner of both the Carnegie Medal
and the Guardian Award in England. In 1978, he was
the "Highly Commended" sole runner-up for the Hans
Christian Andersen Award, given for the outstanding
literary excellence of the entire body of his writing
for children. Mr. Garner and his wife live in a half-
timbered fifteenth century house called Toad Hall in
Blackden-cum-Goostrey in Cheshire, England.